The Reindeer Christmas

BY **MOE PRICE**

ILLUSTRATED BY **ATSUKO MOROZUMI**

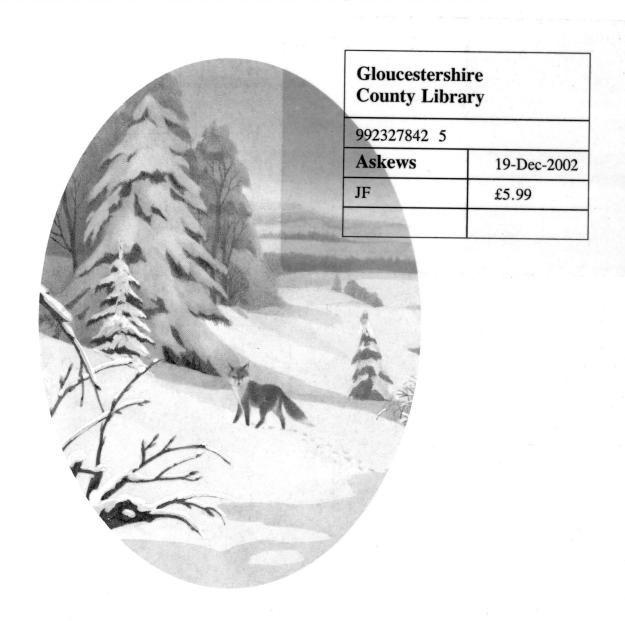

MATHEW PRICE LTD

One Christmas morning, just as dawn was breaking, two
friends hurried through the forest.

"Faster, Elwin," urged Santa Claus. "The sun is coming up.
If anyone sees us, our magic will be lost forever."

The next day Santa Claus and Elwin, his chief elf, sat in front of the fire, sipping their cocoa and toasting their toes.

"Every year there are more homes to visit and more presents to deliver. There just isn't enough time anymore, Elwin," said Santa sadly. "This may be my last Christmas."

"Don't give up, Santa," said Elwin. "There must be a way." They sat in silence, thinking.

Winter was nearly over when Elwin had his wonderful idea.
"Eureka!" he cried. "That's it! That's the answer."

Plans were carefully drawn up.

But then everybody wanted to change them. Sometimes
poor Elwin could hardly hear himself speak.

Finally Elwin got everyone to agree, and soon the workshop was humming with busy, excited elves.

Santa wanted to see what was going on, but the elves would only say, "It's a secret."

At last the secret was revealed. Santa was very impressed. "Elwin," he said, "it's splendid, but . . . I can't pull this big sleigh, not even with you to help me."

Elwin held up his hand.

"An elfin wish have I but one.
I wish it once and then 'tis done.
There's magic in this gift say I,
Whoever pulls this sleigh will fly."

"But who will that be?" asked Santa.

"Don't worry, Santa. We'll find someone to help us. We'll advertise."

WANNTED!
Someone to p...
my sleigh
Christmas Ev...
...reat Rewards...
...ed Santa Cla...

And so they did.

The first to apply for the job was an elephant named Murray.

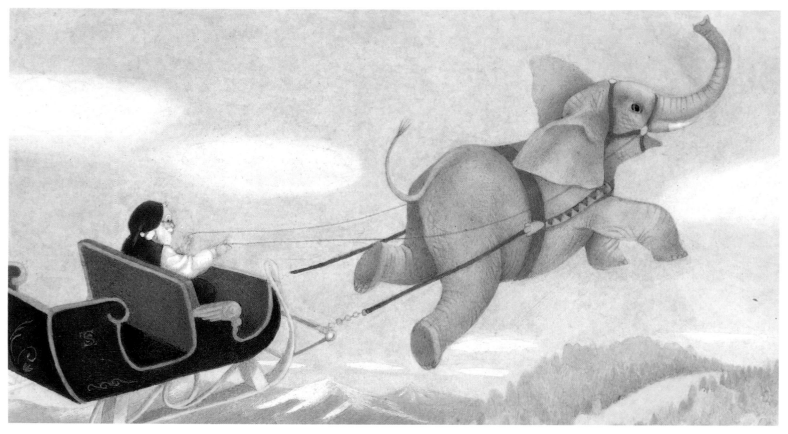

The takeoff was smooth.

And the landing was just perfect.

But Murray didn't get the job.

Next came Marvin the crocodile and some of his friends.

But they all had far too many teeth and looked much too hungry.

Santa Claus was very polite when he turned them down.

Rex, the leader of the huskies, knew his team could do the job. "If you want this sleigh pulled properly," he said, "you need professionals."

Certainly, the takeoff was fast, and the flight was steady.

But then Rex looked down. With a yelp of fear he tried to
climb into the sleigh with Santa. So did everyone else.

The sleigh came to a sudden stop, then fell in swoops and
circles till it sploshed into a large pond.

The day before Christmas a young reindeer knocked on
Santa's door. "One of my friends has fallen into a gorge and
broken his leg," he said. "Can you help us?"

"I'll come at once," said Santa.

"We could use the sleigh for an ambulance," said Elwin.

"That's a good idea," said Santa Claus. "But there's no one to pull it."

"We could," said the reindeer. And that is what they did.

Now Santa Claus knew he could deliver each and every present and still be home before the sun rose on Christmas morning.

And so began a journey that would happen every year until forever.

To Richard and Vincent — A. M.

For Eleanor Doris with all the love
that ever was — M. P.

© text Moe Price 1993
© illustrations Atsuko Morozumi 1993
Designed by Herman Lelie
This edition published 2002 by Mathew Price Ltd
The Old Glove Factory, Bristol Road, Sherborne, Dorset DT9 4HP, UK
All rights reserved
ISBN PB: 1-84248-044-8
ISBN HB: 1-84248-048-0
Printed in Singapore for Imago